Miss Alaineus

A VOCABULARY DISASTER

Written and illustrated by

Debra Frasier

Harcourt, Inc.
San Diego New York London

Aa Bb Cc Dd Ee Ff Gg Hh

With special thanks to the teachers at Marcy Open School, Minneapolis, Minnesota, especially Joanne Toft, Room 202; the teachers at Beachland Elementary, Vero Beach, Florida, both past and present, especially Julie Kotecki and her entire fifth-grade class; and Eleanor Brown, both friend and marvelous teacher

The following people have earned my thanks and extra credit:

The OM team: Maddy, Joseph, Lucy, Sam, Hunter, Ben, and Calla
Hope Kramek for Sheepish
Philip Deaver for Eclectic=Electric
Karrie Oswald for Webster brilliance
Mr. Jefferson Jones for Principal duties

And A+s go to:

Allyn Johnston, for ten years of steadfast confidence and editing
Michael Farmer, book designer of my dreams
Jim Henkel, dear husband and trusted colleague

www.harcourt.com

Library of Congress Cataloging-in-Publication Data
Frasier, Debra.
Miss Alaineus: a vocabulary disaster/by Debra Frasier.
p. cm.
Summary: When Sage's spelling and definition of a word reveal her misunderstanding of it to her classmates, she is at first embarrassed, but then uses her mistake as inspiration for the vocabulary parade.
[1. English language—Spelling—Fiction. 2. Vocabulary—Fiction. 3. Schools—Fiction.] I. Title.
PZ7.F8654Mi 2000
[Fic]—dc21 98-48937
ISBN 0-15-202163-9

Designed by Michael Farmer and Debra Frasier
First edition H G F E D C B A
Printed in Hong Kong

For Calla,
who is not
a cup-shaped lily
growing in the Tropics,
but is, instead,
my fabulous daughter

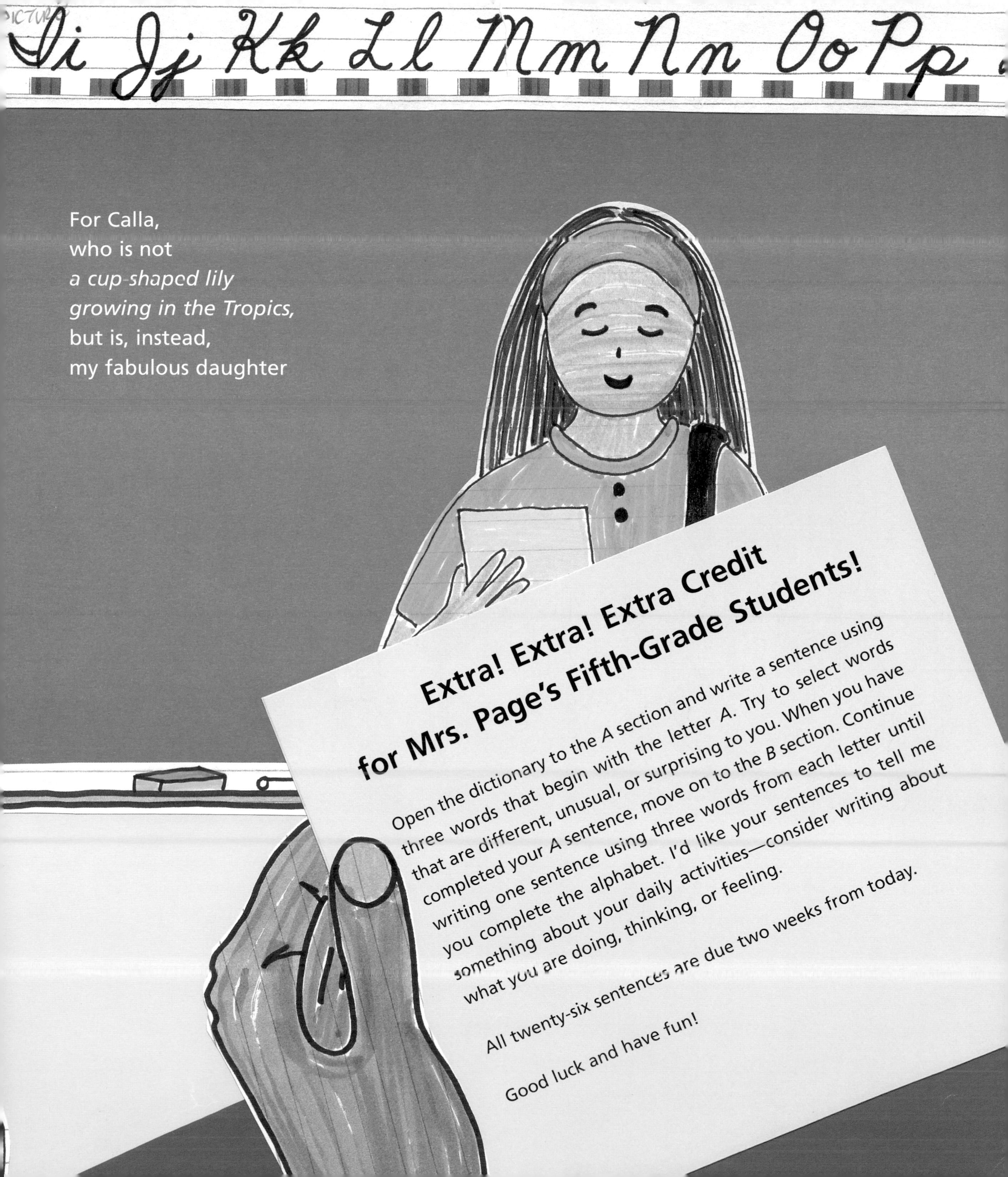

Extra! Extra! Extra Credit for Mrs. Page's Fifth-Grade Students!

Open the dictionary to the *A* section and write a sentence using three words that begin with the letter *A*. Try to select words that are different, unusual, or surprising to you. When you have completed your *A* sentence, move on to the *B* section. Continue writing one sentence using three words from each letter until you complete the alphabet. I'd like your sentences to tell me something about your daily activities—consider writing about what you are doing, thinking, or feeling.

All twenty-six sentences are due two weeks from today.

Good luck and have fun!

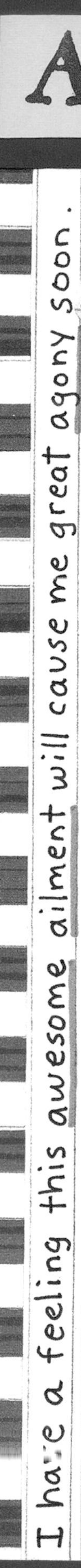

None of this would have happened if it wasn't for Forest. Forest is not *a thicket of trees.* Forest is a boy. A sick boy. A boy sneezing and coughing all over my desk and pencils.

I caught Forest's cold and had to stay home from school on Tuesday. Tuesday is Vocabulary Day at Webster School. Follow my advice: Never get sick on Vocabulary Day.

On Tuesday afternoon I called my best friend, Starr, who is not *a luminous celestial object seen as a point of light in the sky,* but a very smart girl who listens perfectly on Vocabulary Day. She was late for baseball practice, so she spelled the first fourteen vocabulary words as fast as she could.

I had to scribble them quickly because her mom was calling her to the car. "The last one's 'Miss Alaineus'!" Starr yelled. "I gotta go. I hope you feel better tomorrow, Sage." And she hung up the phone with a crash.

VOCABULARY WORDS

1. dinosaur
2. snake
3. museum
4. reptile
5. constrictor
6. herpetologist
7. fossil
8. carnivore
9. herbivore
10. nest
11. species
12. theory
13. hypothesis
14. category
15. Miss Alainous

I didn't feel much better on Wednesday, so my mom called Mrs. Page, who is not *a single side of a printed sheet of paper usually found bound in a book.* She's my teacher, and actually Mrs. Page is a good name for her because she reads to us every day. My mom told her yes, I had my math problems and vocabulary words, and yes, I would get better soon.

Every week Mrs. Page gives us a list of words with a theme, like Story Writing or Musical Performance or Electricity. We're supposed to look up each word in the dictionary, but sometimes I already know the words, so I try to make the definitions sound like I looked them up.

C I croak when I cough, and I call this a terrible catastrophe. C

tree: a large leafy plant with a tall wooden trunk that pushes roots into the ground and branches into the sky

automobile: a vehicle, used to transport humans, usually consisting of four wheels, a steering wheel, and a radio

I thought I was pretty good at definitions until this week. My mom says, "Pride goeth before a fall."

Pride: *an unduly high opinion of oneself.*

Goeth: *Old English for "to go."*

Fall: *what happened on Monday, Vocabulary Test Day.*

I am defective and delirious, and soon I will dwindle away.

By Thursday afternoon my head felt like it was stuffed with cotton and my throat felt swollen shut. I finished defining my vocabulary words while propped up in bed with a box of tissues on one side and a gigantic red dictionary on the other. It's hard to look up words in a huge book while you're in bed blowing your nose, so I made my own dictionary language for as many of them as I could.

13. hypothesis: what you guess will happen in your science experiment
14. category: a bunch of things that are alike
15. Miss Alaineus:

The last word seemed a little odd to me because I couldn't figure out what she had to do with snakes or categories or theories. Mrs. Page rarely gives us people's names on our vocabulary lists, but we have had a few that turned into words, like Louis Pasteur for **pasteurization** and George Washington for **Washington, D.C.,** so I decided she must have been included for a reason.

E Can I endure this extraordinary redness in my eyeballs? E

F
This burning fever makes my future look dim and fuzzy.
F

You should know that for years I had wondered who Miss Alaineus was. When I was little I figured out that she had something to do with the kitchen, because the Miss Alaineus drawer held the spoons too big to fit anywhere else, the sharp corn holders shaped like tiny cobs, and the spaghetti spork, that weird cross between a spoon and a fork that perfectly lifts slippery spaghetti out of the bowl. I thought maybe she was an **ancestor:** *an ancient relative long dead,* who left us all these odd things in the drawer.

Then just last year my mom and I were at the grocery store and it all fell into place. We were in one of those Very Big Hurries when she said, "You go get some of that long Italian bread and two sticks of butter. I'll get Miss Alaineus' things and meet you here at the cash register."

I found the bread and butter, and my mom came back with spaghetti sauce, a can of Parmesan cheese, a can of corn, and a big green box of spaghetti with a beautiful woman on the front. She was drawn so that her hair tumbled perfectly across the box and ended in a little plastic window, making the spaghetti look just like the ends of the strands of her hair.

There she was—Miss Alaineus.

G Can't you hear my gloomy groans and gruesome wails? G

Won't this heap of homework make my headache worse?

So, propped up on pillows in my bed, with a tissue in one hand and a pencil in the other, I wrote:

15. Miss Alaineus: the woman on green spaghetti boxes whose hair is the color of uncooked pasta

and turns into spaghetti at the ends

And then I fell asleep.

I If I don't improve soon, insanity is inevitable. I

and turns into spaghetti at the ends
SPAGHETTI
FINE
FINE
J
My bed is just a jumbo jumble of germy sheets.
J

K Aa Bb Cc Dd Ee Ff Gg H

Did this ailment kick my years of knowledge back to Kindergarten?

I finally got better over the weekend and felt great on Monday. I turned in my homework to Mrs. Page and sat down at my desk, glad to be back at school with my friends. I was even glad to see Forest at our morning circle meeting.

"First, I want to remind you of the Tenth Annual Vocabulary Parade on Friday," said Mrs. Page. "I hope you are all working on your word costumes. Second, please remember to bring your bus money and permission slips for our science museum field trip tomorrow. And third, instead of our usual Monday test, we are going to have a Vocabulary Bee today.

"Everyone line up here by the chalkboard, and I'll choose

Ii Jj Kk Ll Mm Nn Oo

L

Is it likely a bit of learning was lost each time I blew my nose?

a word from our list. After I pronounce the word, please spell and define it. If you are correct, go to the end of the line. If you miss the word, please sit down at your desk and look it up in the dictionary. Write the word five times and define it once."

Starr was first with **museum**: **"M-U-S-E-U-M:** *a building for exhibiting objects about art or history or science,"* she said, and went to the back of the line.

Cliff, not *a high, steep face of rock,* but one very tall boy, answered to the word **dinosaur**: **"D-I-N-O-S-A-U-R:** *a prehistoric, extinct reptile, often huge,"* and he went to the back of the line.

L

I was tenth, and when Mrs. Page called out my word, I spelled: "Capital **M-I-S-S,** capital **A-L-A-I-N-E-U-S,**" and added, *"the woman on green spaghetti boxes whose hair is the color of uncooked pasta and turns into spaghetti at the ends."*

There was a moment of silence in the room. I smiled at Mrs. Page. She waited to see if I would add anything else, and when I didn't, she grinned. Not smiled—**grinned:** *to draw back the lips and bare the teeth, as in a very wide smile*—and the entire class burst into one huge giggling, laughing, falling-down mass of kids. Forest was doubled over. Starr, my best friend, was laughing so hard tears came to her eyes. By now, even Mrs. Page was laughing.

Pride goeth before a fall. I was **Sage:** *one who shows wisdom, experience, judgment.* Why were they laughing? "Wise-girl-with-words" my dad always called me. What had I said? I was beginning to turn red. **Red:** *the color of embarrassment.*

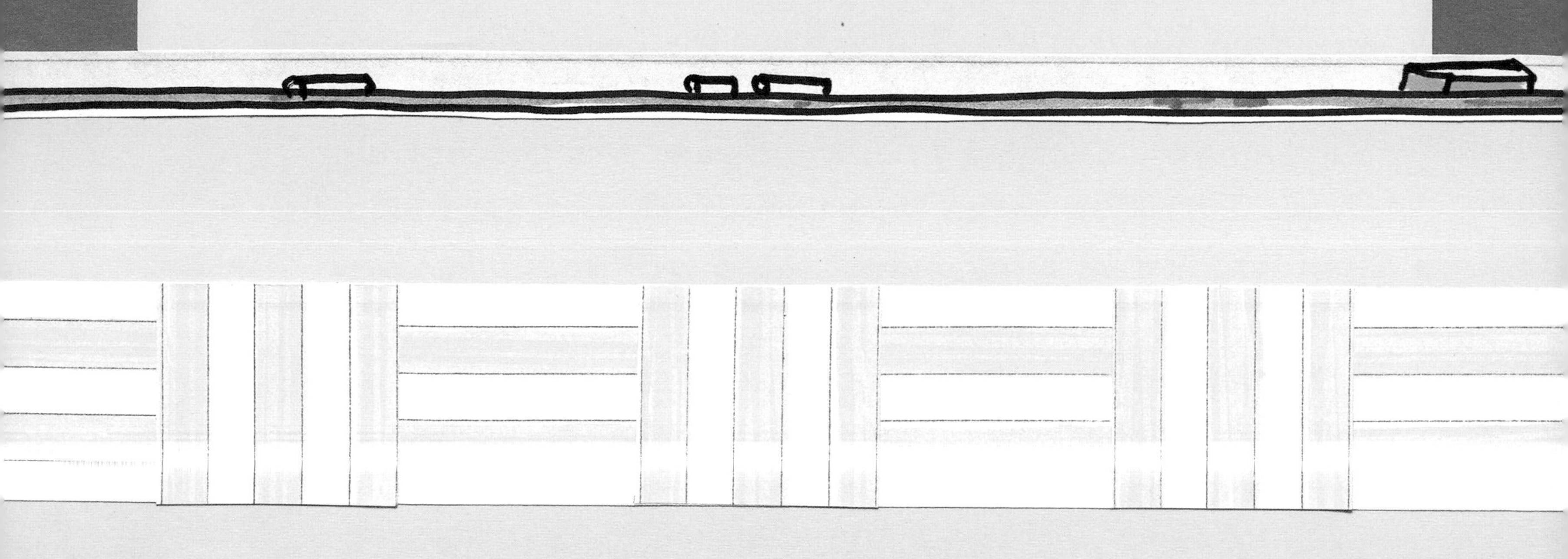

Did I mention that my moaning, mournful days are over?

Math : 9:30
Music
Journal
Forest
Hope
Cliff ✓
N
Did you see that my turn is near and I'm not even nervous?
N

Finally the room quieted. Mrs. Page opened her dictionary and wrote on the chalkboard:

> **Miscellaneous**: *adj. 1. consisting of various kinds or qualities 2. a collection of unrelated objects*

My jaw dropped as I looked at the spelling. My eyes bulged as I read the definition. I didn't bother to tell anyone about my mom and the spaghetti spork and the grocery store. **Humbled:** *aware of my shortcomings, modest, meek,* I dragged back to my seat and wrote **miscellaneous** five times and defined it once. And that's when I remembered I had even drawn a picture of the spaghetti box for extra credit. I was **devastated:** *wasted, ravaged.* **Ruined:** *destroyed.* **Finished:** *brought to an end.*

They called me Miss Alaineus for the rest of the day. Sometimes a person couldn't even get the words out before bending over with laughter. The day took a week to end. When I got off the bus I slumped home—devastated, ruined, finished.

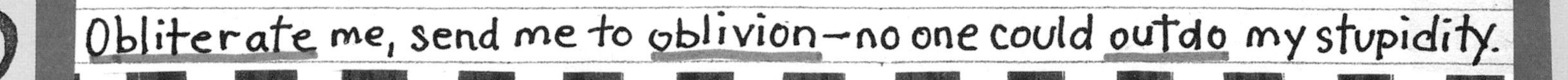

Cc Dd Ee Ff Gg Hh Ii
Miscellaneous: adj.
1. consisting of various kinds or qualities
2. a collection of unrelated objects
P
This is positively the most painful day of my short, pathetic life.
P

I told my mom the whole story, from the kitchen drawer to the grocery store to the Vocabulary Bee. Even my own mother laughed a little at the part about the drawing for extra credit, but at least she stopped fast and said, "You know what I always say...There's gold in every mistake."

Gold? *A bright yellow precious metal of great value?*

Mistake? *Something done, said, or thought in the wrong way?*

"Impossible," I told her. **Impossible:** *not capable of happening.*

I couldn't believe I *ever* had to go back to school. But the next day we went to the science museum, and everyone forgot all about Miss Alaineus at the snake exhibit and the dinosaur bone lab. Then the guide said, "The field of bone archaeology has been influenced by a wide and unusual array of miscellaneous discoveries around the world." The class burst out laughing, and the guide was pleased with herself for entertaining us so easily. And I **knew:** *to apprehend with certainty,* that my mistake was still alive and well, and nothing like gold.

With one quiet question my life sank into quicksand.

On this ruined, rotten day, it rains in my heart.

After school I lay on my bed and stared at the wall. How could I have been so stupid?

My mom came in and said it was time to work on my costume for the Vocabulary Parade. We had finished the cape for **Capable,** but I still needed to make the lettering down the back.

"Mom," I said, "I could only be a mistake this year. **Miss Stake.**"

S Will I feel better someday, somewhere, somehow? S

Suddenly I sat up.
I looked at my mom.
She looked at me.
I smiled.
She smiled.
"Sweetheart," she said, "let's take another look at that cape."

U

Undaunted, I undertook those unforgettable steps onto the stage.

It took the most courage I've ever had to walk out on that stage as **Miss Alaineus,** *Queen of All Miscellaneous Things.* But when Mr. Bell read my word and definition, everyone applauded and laughed **wildly:** *in a manner lacking all restraint,* and I grinned at my mom across the auditorium.

Forest came right after me. When he bowed, his **Precipitation** watering-can hat rained on Mr. Bell's new suit, and the entire audience gasped, then cheered when Mr. Bell smiled at his soggy clothes.

The stage was vast, I felt valiant, and no one threw a vegetable.

We waved and whistled and wished it would never end.

To my **astonishment:** *great shock and amazement,* I won a gold trophy for The Most Original Use of a Word in the Tenth Annual Vocabulary Parade.

So this time Mom was right. There *was* gold in this mistake.

And next year I think I'm going to be...

X
If x = happy, then we were all x × 10 and chiming like xylophones.
X
MISS ALAINEUS
QUEEN OF ALL MISCELLANEOUS THINGS
GIFT
ORBIT
A UN
TEDECTS
A COLLECT

Y Over yonder you'll see me jump and yell with glee! Y

MYSTERIOUS

Full of mystery...Hard to explain or understand

Miss Sterious, *Investigator of All Things Mysterious!*

Z I'll zip my backpack and zoom with zest right out of here.

Sage's Vocabulary Parade Scrapbook

KINDERGARTEN

FIRST GRADE

SECOND GRADE

Every year my mom and I make a costume together.

In Kindergarten I filled my boots with water and it was a terrible mess.

In Fourth Grade Starr and I got our idea from Mrs. Brown when she said, "You two girls stick to each other like magnets!"

Dear Students and Parents:

We hope to see you all at our annual Vocabulary Parade at 7 P.M. next Friday. Refreshments will follow the parade, as usual. (Please contact Mrs. Brown in Room 101 about bringing something for the refreshment table.) If you have any questions, please direct them to me in Room 202. I can't wait to see what our students will create!

Sincerely,

Joanne Page

Joanne Page, Vocabulary Parade Committee

Webster School's Tenth Annual Vocabulary Parade Rules

The all-school, all-grade vocabulary lists for this year have been posted outside the library. You may choose a word from any list. Once you have made your selection, write your room number next to the word. Note that you are not limited to these words and may add a word of your own selection to the list. Your costume can be any creative interpretation of your word. If it is best displayed and defined by more than one person, you may work in teams of up to three people. Remember to include your chosen vocabulary word on the costume somewhere.

Each student must turn in a 3×5" card to his or her teacher BY THURSDAY, with the following information: (1) your name, grade, and room number; (2) vocabulary word; (3) definition; and (4) a sentence describing some aspect of your costume if you think it will help your performance.

As usual, Mr. Bell will read these cards during our parade, so PLEASE PRINT CLEARLY. If you want to say your own definition as part of your performance, please note that on the top of your card.

Happy Defining!

FOURTH GRADE

1) Sage 5th Grade Rm 202

2) miscellaneous

3) 1. consisting of various kinds or qualities
2. a collection of unrelated objects

4) There are over 100 miscellaneous objects on this costume.

MR. BELL AND ME

BACK VIEW WITH MOM

In Fifth Grade my disaster turned to gold!

FOREST SPILLING AGAIN!

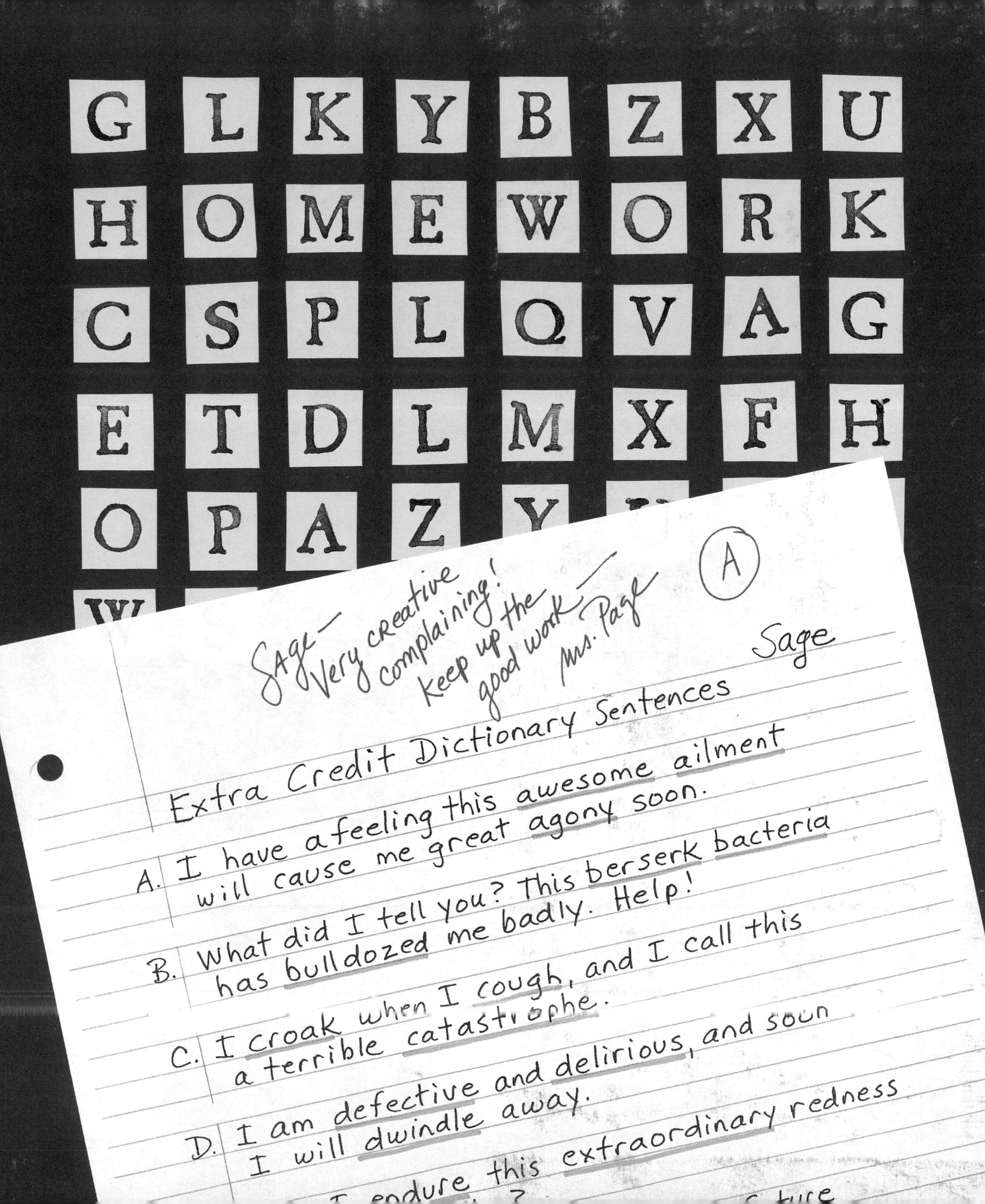
G L K Y B Z X U
H O M E W O R K
C S P L Q V A G
E T D L M X F H
O P A Z
Sage— Very creative complaining! Keep up the good work— Ms. Page
A
Sage
Extra Credit Dictionary Sentences
A. I have a feeling this awesome ailment will cause me great agony soon.
B. What did I tell you? This berserk bacteria has bulldozed me badly. Help!
C. I croak when I cough, and I call this a terrible catastrophe.
D. I am defective and delirious, and soon I will dwindle away.
I endure this extraordinary redness